S0-ANP-369

A Note to Parents and Caregivers:

Read-it! Readers are for children who are just starting on the amazing road to reading. These beautiful books support both the acquisition of reading skills and the love of books.

The PURPLE LEVEL presents basic topics and objects using high frequency words and simple language patterns.

The RED LEVEL presents familiar topics using common words and repeating sentence patterns.

The BLUE LEVEL presents new ideas using a larger vocabulary and varied sentence structure.

The YELLOW LEVEL presents more challenging ideas, a broad vocabulary, and wide variety in sentence structure.

The GREEN LEVEL presents more complex ideas, an extended vocabulary range, and expanded language structures.

The ORANGE LEVEL presents a wide range of ideas and concepts using challenging vocabulary and complex language structures.

When sharing a book with your child, read in short stretches, pausing often to talk about the pictures. Have your child turn the pages and point to the pictures and familiar words. And be sure to reread favorite stories or parts of stories.

There is no right or wrong way to share books with children. Find time to read with your child, and pass on the legacy of literacy.

Adria F. Klein, Ph.D.
Professor Emeritus
California State University
San Bernardino, California

First American edition published in 2005 by
Picture Window Books
5115 Excelsior Boulevard
Suite 232
Minneapolis, MN 55416
877-845-8392
www.picturewindowbooks.com

First published in Canada in 1999 by
Les éditions Héritage inc.
300 Arran Street, Saint Lambert
Quebec, Canada J4R 1K5

Printed in the United States of America.

Library of Congress Cataloging-in-Publication Data
St-Aubin, Bruno.
Daddy's an alien / Bruno St-Aubin.
p. cm. — (Read-it! readers)
Summary: After a child's father returns from an airplane trip looking different and acting strangely, his family begins to suspect that he may be an alien.
ISBN 1-4048-1067-6 (hardcover)
[1. Fathers—Fiction. 2. Extraterrestrial beings—Fiction. 3. Humorous stories.] I. Title: Daddy is an alien. II. Title. III. Series.

PZ7.S7743Dah 2004
[Fic]—dc22 2004024428

Daddy's an Alien

Written and Illustrated by
Bruno St-Aubin

Special thanks to our advisers for their expertise:

Adria F. Klein, Ph.D.
Professor Emeritus, California State University
San Bernardino, California

Susan Kesselring, M.A.
Literacy Educator
Rosemount - Apple Valley - Eagan (Minnesota) School District

I like school, cabbage soup, and my clothes neatly put away.

I also like classical music and my little brother.

Do you think I'm pretty normal?

Wait until you see my dad!

Since his last airplane trip, he is not
the same.

You could say that he lives on a cloud.

He lets everything drag behind him.

He's a real tornado!

He loves French fries and really hot candy.

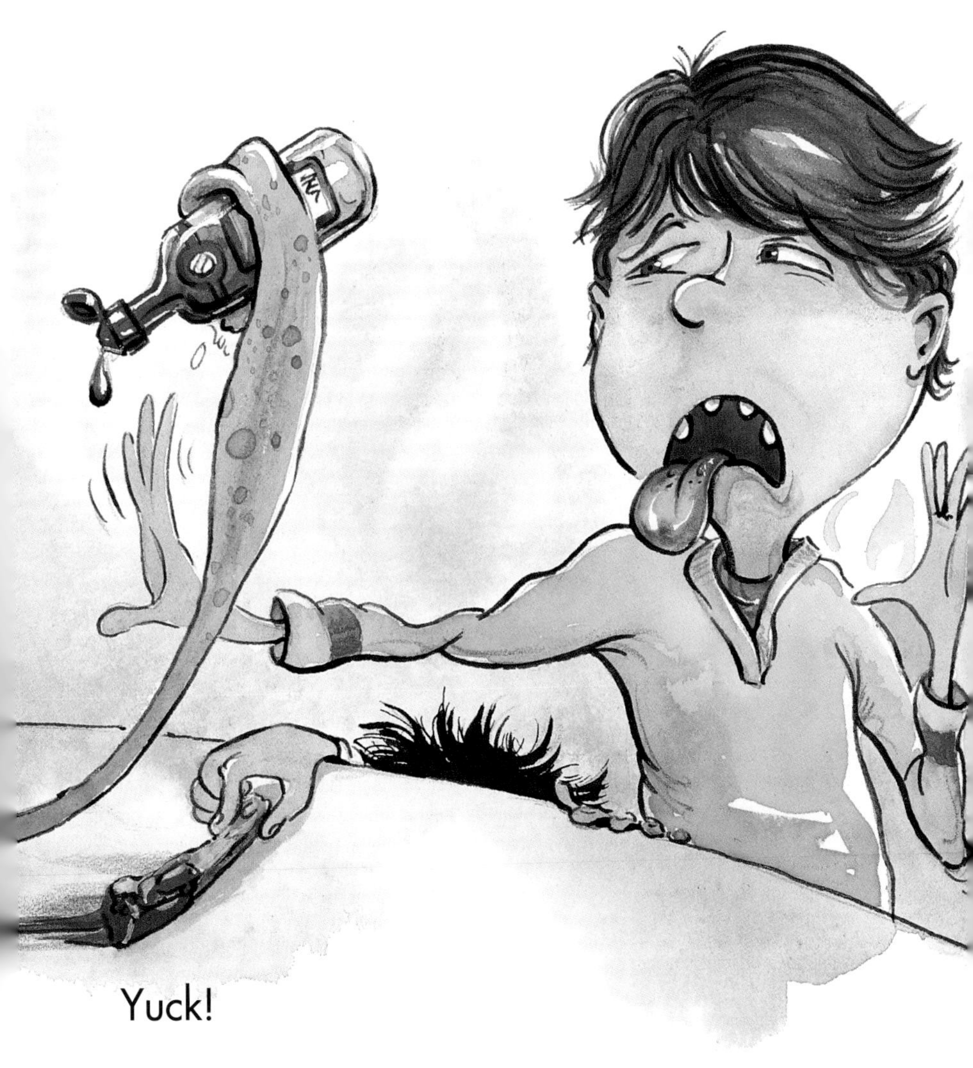

Yuck!

He listens to strange space music
that is totally worthless.

Yuck!

When he wants to help me do
my homework,

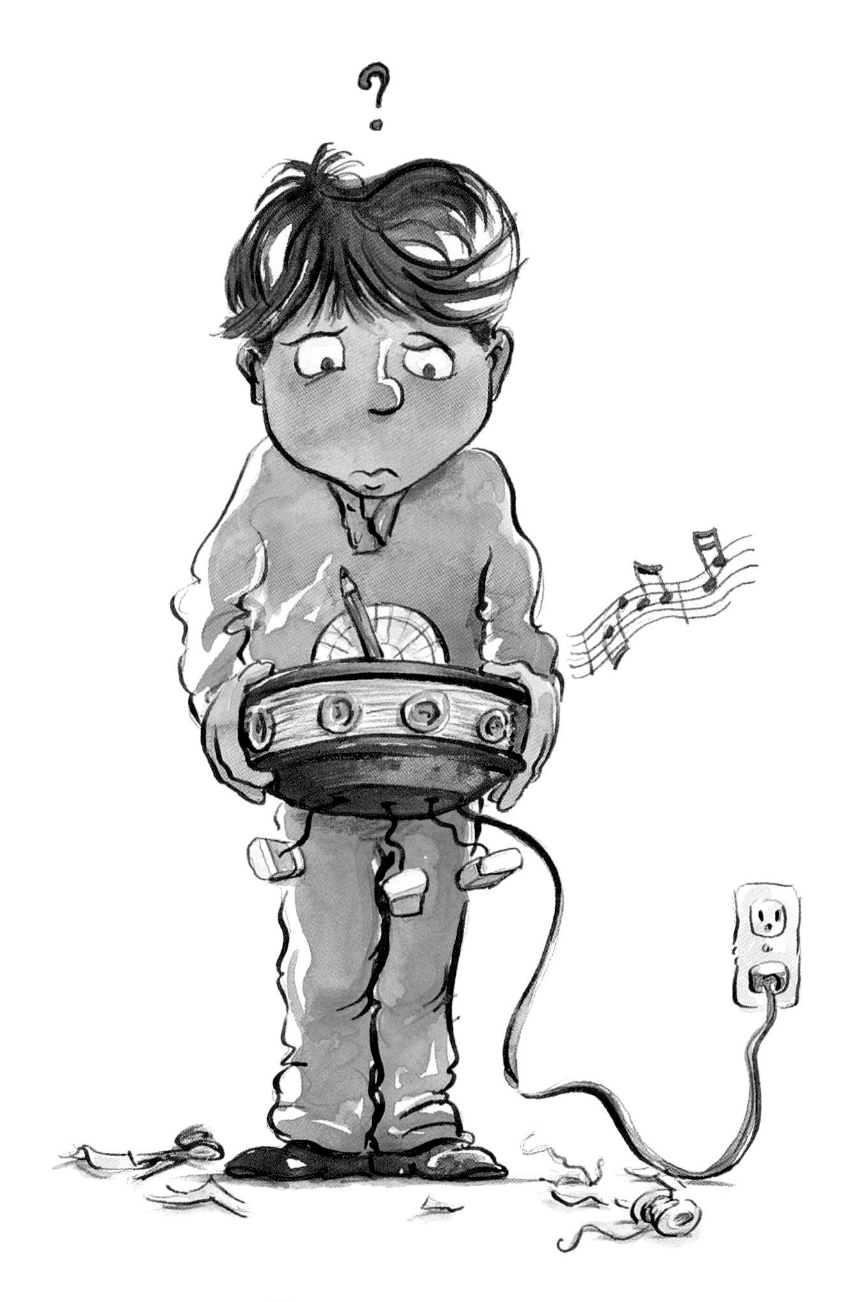

he messes it all up.

Sometimes, Mom gets discouraged,

especially when he does the housework!

Dad likes to do the grocery shopping.

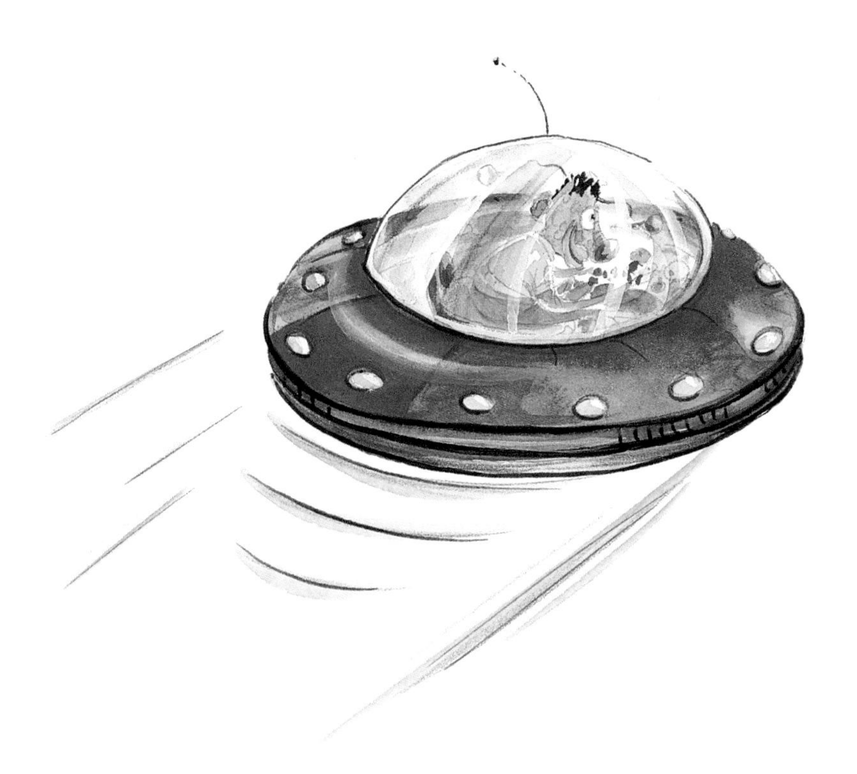

The other day, he bought himself an
extra-sporty super flying saucer.

Then he came to visit me at school.

How embarrassing!

He talked to the whole class about his job as a toy inventor.

All my friends loved him.

It's true that he's awesome at soccer ...

just not in our living room!

Dad was really sorry.

To apologize, he climbed into
the washing machine.

He came out completely changed!

I am glad to see him finally be a little more normal ...

But for how long?

More *Read-it!* Readers

Bright pictures and fun stories help you practice your reading skills. Look for more books at your level.

A Clown in Love by Mireille Villeneuve
Alex and the Game of the Century by Gilles Tibo
Alex and Toolie by Gilles Tibo
Daddy's an Alien by Bruno St-Aubin
Emily Lee Carole Temblay
Forrest and Freddy by Gilles Tibo
Gabby's School by the Sea by Marie-Danielle Croteau
Grampy's Bad Day by Dominique Demers
John's Day by Marie-Francine Hébert
Peppy, Patch, and the Postman by Marisol Sarrazin
Peppy, Patch, and the Socks by Marisol Sarrazin
The Princess and the Frog by Margaret Nash
Rachel's Adventure Ring by Sylvia Roberge Blanchet
Run! by Sue Ferraby
Sausages! by Anne Adeney
Stickers, Shells, and Snow Globes by Dana Meachen Rau
Theodore the Millipede by Carole Tremblay
The Truth About Hansel and Gretel by Karina Law
When Nobody's Looking ... by Louise Tondreau-Levert

Looking for a specific title or level? A complete list of *Read-it!* Readers is available on our Web site: *www.picturewindowbooks.com*